CAVE OF COURAGE

ESCAPING THE MASHUPS

Kim Andrascik

ISBN 978-1-62806-339-4   (print | paperback)

Library of Congress Control Number 2021923197

Published by Salt Water Media
29 Broad Street, Suite 104
Berlin, MD 21811
www.saltwatermedia.com

Cover art and interior illustrations by Kendall Royer
Editing by Bill Cecil

DEDICATION

To my two creative, smart, kind,
and courageous children, Sky and Saylor.

And their "siblings" Khloe and Kamden.

And to my supportive husband,
parents (my heroes), sister, and family.

And my wonderful friends of many years -
Greavers, Tita, Keith, Dan,
Allison (friend and family), Jess.

CONTENTS

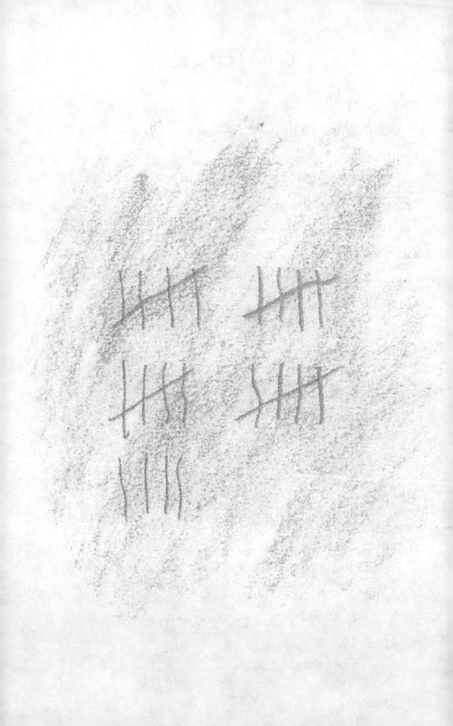

CHAPTER 1

NIGHT 24 IN THE CAVE

While the fire provided warmth and light, Sky and May felt a cold chill deep in their bones and dark thoughts continued to swirl around like a spinning top. They used memories of their life before the mashups to remind them of the laughter and lessons of their past. Collecting memories and searching for little rays of sunshine in this new world became a part of their survival routine. The thought of collecting memories made Sky smile as he recalled spending hours playing the video game *Unravel*. The game followed the character Yarny as he collected memories in a ravaged world. Sky felt a little bit like Yarny. As his mind drifted to days of endless hours gaming, he was abruptly interrupted by May.

"When are Mom and Dad coming back?" May asked Sky while glancing at the cave wall where white chalk marks were used as a primitive calendar. Sky did his best to disguise his growing concern. "May, you keep asking and the answer is the same, they will be back soon. It takes time to gather supplies and avoid the mashups. Don't you remember how long it took us to walk to this cave from our old home with our bags at night without being found?" May looked down. She did remember that terrible night when they packed what they could carry and walked for miles to the cave.

The cave looked like a hole cut in the side of the rocky steep cliff overlooking the ocean. According to Dad, he noticed the cave while fishing for rockfish and flounder a year earlier. After spotting the cave, Dad discovered it could be accessed by carefully following a slippery, rocky trail weaving down the wall of the cliff. Dad was a rock climber so the climb was easy for him. He was nervous the first time he went into the cave and half expected a wild animal to maul him when he entered. Instead, he found a small empty cave about 500 square feet in size. He realized the cave would have been impossible for animals to access as it was a forty-foot hard climb down the cliff from land and would have required a twenty-foot climb up from the sea. Because of the dangerous climb, Dad did not take anyone else to the cliffside cave until it became a necessity a year after he discovered it.

CHAPTER 2

FIRST NIGHT IN THE CAVE

Sky was more hesitant than May for the climb down. At seven years old, May was tough and always up for a challenge. When she was thrown from a horse, she would jump right back on. Even though Sky was her older brother at ten years old, he was very analytical and weighed the costs and benefits before jumping into something. May looked up to Sky and was amazed at his knowledge. While Sky was always impressed and envious of May's strength and refusal to back down without a fight, it did, at times, result in some arguments between them.

On this particular night there was no talking, let alone arguing. Everyone was scared and tired. Dad knew it was important for everyone to stay calm and alert to ensure a safe climb. He looked at Mom, Sky and May, "I know everyone is exhausted and nervous

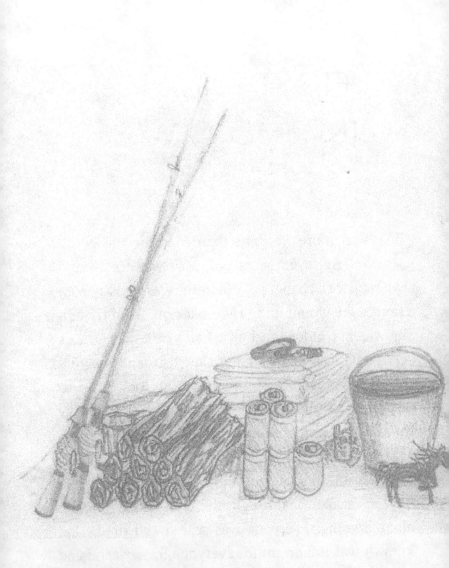

for the climb. Whatever you do, remember the lessons and safety tips I taught you on other climbs. You need to stay relaxed and focused. I prepared the equipment and ropes to make the climb and cave access as easy as possible. We can do this!" Sky and May were not convinced and looked at each other with worry.

May went first. Her blue eyes narrowed in concentration and she steadied her breathing. After counting to three, she started her descent. Other than a minor slip and scraped knee, she made it down safely. Sky was next. He imagined one of his favorite video games, Little Nightmares. In the game, a girl named Six climbs and jumps to avoid crazy creatures. Sky felt a little like Six scaling the cliff. He summoned all his courage and started down the cliff. His confidence grew as he realized he was safe with the ropes and was strong enough to make the climb. Once safely inside the cave, it was Mom's turn, but they were nervous for her climb. Mom was always the one that would trip or spill something. Under normal circumstances, Mom's minor accidents were good for a laugh. In this case, a minor accident could mean catastrophe. Mom put on a brave face for Sky and May and tried to control her shaking. Sky and May watched anxiously as Mom worked very slowly down to the cave. When she made it, they cheered and hugged. Sky, May and Mom carefully looked out the cave to see Dad expertly scale down and enter the cave. He made it look so easy.

With everyone safe and sound in the cave, May smiled proudly and announced that she was a faster climber than Mom and Sky. Sky smirked and informed May, "You may be faster but at least I didn't scrape my knee. I am more careful than you and that makes me a better climber."

May glared at Sky and opened her mouth to object but Mom quickly chimed in, "You are both amazing and brave kids and great climbers. I know we are all tired but if we work together, we can unpack quickly and then sleep." May and Sky slowly nodded in agreement.

While Dad made several trips that night to and from the cave with items the family packed in bags, Mom, Sky and May got to work in the cave. The trio took out blankets, wood, food, lighters, water, drink mix packets, buckets, clothes, medicine, knives, fishing poles, games, paper, pens, chalk, walkie-talkies, batteries, personal desalination bottles, and other items Mom and Dad had packed. May unpacked a few Breyer horses to play with and Sky had his art supplies and battery-operated headphones. Everyone was exhausted and slept soundly the first night by the fire.

CHAPTER 3

MASHUPS

Upon waking that first morning in the cave, the family took in the amazing views of the ocean raging below and the dizzying steep drop down the cliff to the rocks below. This would be an incredible place for an overnight camping trip. Unfortunately, this was not a vacation and they didn't know how long they would be here. This uncertainty resulted in a variety of questions from May that first morning. "Mom, how long will we be in here? When can I go home? Are we safe in here? Where did the mashups come from and when will they go away?" While these questions had all been answered by Mom and Dad before, they knew May needed to hear them again to put her at ease. Sky wanted to hear the answers again as well to hone in on any discrepancies in the answers from Mom and Dad and see if they were

telling the entire truth. He knew they sometimes sugar-coated things.

Mom looked at May and then to the ocean as if drawing in courage from the raging sea and slowly began to answer the questions. "May, we don't know how long we will be here or how long until we go home. We have enough supplies to last a long time in the cave and there are plenty more supplies we can gather if we need to. The cave is safe from the mashups. Home is wherever we are all together. It doesn't matter what it looks like as long as we have each other." Mom stopped speaking for a moment to gather her thoughts and Sky was on high alert to hear the explanation of the mashups. Mom began again. "Two years ago, a laboratory called DNAnimals Inc. began combining genes of various animals to engineer the perfect pet. People would pay thousands of dollars to the lab and then select the type, size, color, life span, energy level, climate tolerance, skills, intelligence, likes, dislikes, and any other characteristic you can imagine to create the perfect pet."

May interrupted, "What is wrong with that? I would love to create a horse my size that lives forever and is black and white with blue eyes and can jump higher than any other horse. I could even design horses for all my friends. Then we would all compete in horse shows together and win ribbons. We could even do barrel racing in a rodeo."

Sky rolled his eyes and cut her off as he knew she could go on forever about horses. "May! Stop talking about stupid horses and let Mom finish!" he yelled.

May narrowed her eyes and yelled back, "Squealer, all you care about are stupid creepy video games, and I know who you have a crush on and can't wait to tell everyone!" May knew calling her brother "Squealer" and threatening to spill his secrets would make him angry. Before it could escalate, Dad intervened and threatened that Mom wouldn't continue unless they stopped arguing. He explained that fighting and arguing in a cave could end up with someone hurt or falling to the rocks below. This resulted temporarily in a truce and Mom continued.

"At first, the pets created at the lab were cats and dogs with minor genetic mutations to create characteristics like a longer life span, improved health, and intelligence. However, as more money funneled into the lab, the mutations and requests became more extreme. Driven by demand and money, the scientists scrambled to piece together genes to create more extreme hybrids. Some people wanted fantasy-like creatures such as dog-horse hybrids, cat-dog hybrids, rabbit-dog hybrids, and rabbit-cat hybrids. However, more sinister requests spawned the creation of hybrids to use as weapons."

With a confused expression, May asked Mom, "What is sinister?"

Mom explained, "Sinister means evil or harmful." Sky sighed. He just wanted to hear the rest of the story. May always had questions.

Mom continued, "As more and more hybrids were created and the scientists perfected various mutations, the type of animals became more and more advanced. It was like hundreds of years of evolution took place in a matter of months. Unfortunately, the hybrids that seemed to thrive and breed and outsmart all others were the most dangerous and aggressive types. The weaponized hybrids began to outlive, outsmart, and outbreed all other hybrids. They grew in number from two to hundreds to thousands in no time. Herds started to take over large spans of land. These massive herds drove out the existing animal populations and destroyed crops, creating drastic changes in the ecosystem. Shortages of food and land began to emerge, and humans began attempts to fight back the herds. At this point, the government attempted to intervene by hunting and exterminating the hybrids.

May asked, "What is "extermination"?

Sky rolled his eyes, "May, are you kidding me? It means kill, murder, or execute. Think of what I do to your character in every video game. I destroy your weak characters."

Mom cut him off, "Sky, be nice to your sister. It's good she has questions. That's why she is so smart. By the way, I recall May beating you in a few video games." May smiled. She loved when Sky got in trouble.

Sky was annoyed, "Mom, I am always nice to May. I am so nice that I let her win games sometimes. Will you please finish the story?"

Mom continued, "As thousands were killed, the remaining hybrids continued to fight, and some went into hiding. These remaining hybrids became known as mashups and banded together in a pursuit of survival and elimination of their biggest threat, humans."

May was anxious for Mom to answer the most important part of her question and asked again, "When will the mashups go away?". Sky let this question slide because he wanted to know the answer too.

Mom knew this answer was important to the kids and she responded carefully, "The scientists and government are working on an extermination plan for the mashups, but we don't know how long that will take. It is a difficult mission and extremely hard to distinguish between mashups and other animals.

Mashups have become very adept at survival and sometimes hide among other animals."

Sky chimed in, "Are you sure the mash-ups can't reach our cave?" Dad assured him, "The mashups are not adapted to climbing cliffs or living by the ocean. They also can't see or hear us here with the ocean crashing. I promise, we are safe here."

Sky hoped and prayed Dad was right. While Sky and May encountered many friendly hybrids over the past year, their first sighting of a dangerous mashup was the previous morning before leaving their house for the cave. Unlike the friendly dog-cats, horse-dogs, rabbit-cats, and other unique hybrids Sky and May would see in the street, meet at their friend's house, and "oohhh" and "aahhh" over, the mashups Sky saw through his window the prior morning looked like rabid monsters. He could see thousands in the farmer's field across the canal through his binoculars. The mashups had jagged huge teeth, yellowish eyes, bodies the size of a large pony but with a head like a wolf or husky. They had cat-like razor sharp claws that seemed to protrude from hoof-like feet. Their pitch-black fur was coated in mud and matted with something oily. When they weren't grazing or tearing down trees, violent fights would break out.

From this first sighting, Sky created drawings of the mashups to add to his personal journal. He filled this journal with his artwork, stories, and video game strategies. In addition to drawings of the mashups, he also decided to name the mashups by type in his journal. He labelled the initial mashup he witnessed from his house "Black Wolf". It seemed fitting and reminded him of another favorite video game, Minecraft. In Minecraft Dungeons, Black Wolf armor was used to protect against attacks. Sky wasn't yet sure what he could use to avoid an attack by a Black Wolf, but for now he used his imagination and thought of Black Wolf armor. Sky couldn't help wishing the mashups were just villains in a video game and that this entire nightmare was just a hard level to solve.

Dad and Mom also saw the herd across the canal that morning. All that separated their house from the mashups was a narrow canal. Mom and Dad knew the mashups would figure out how to go around the canal if they needed more food or land or sensed humans were close to their new territory. Knowing danger was so close, Mom and Dad set their plan in motion to pack up and move the family to the cave that night.

CHAPTER 4

INSIDE THE CAVE

After a few days in the cave, everyone started to settle into a survival routine. There were pillows and blankets for sleeping around the fire in the cave at night. The fire kept the cave very warm at night and provided light to read and play games. Even without a fire at night, the cave rarely dipped below 60 degrees. During the day, the cave was much warmer thanks to the heat from the strong summer sun. The cave offered shade from the sun and shelter from rain and wind. At night, the sound of the ocean, the warmth of the fire, and pure exhaustion from the daily survival routine combined to lure the family into sleep. May and Sky sometimes woke at night after a scary nightmare. On many nights, May, Sky, and Mom woke to the loud sounds of Dad's snoring. The sound would echo through the cave and Sky and May would wake up giggling.

As Sky and May woke each morning, Mom would prepare breakfast on the fire. Usually oatmeal and canned fruit. Sky and May loved when Mom would make a pitcher of lemonade using Crystal Light lemonade mix packets and water to drink with breakfast. However, as the drink mix supply was limited, everyone mostly drank plain water. Dad had packed all four of them a personal water filter and desalination device to turn the salt water into drinkable water.

After breakfast Dad, Sky, and May would use the ropes and ladder Dad placed on the cliff to scale from the cave down to the rocks by the ocean. Once down, Dad would fill a bucket with sea water and use a pulley he had set up to transport the water

to the cave. Mom would untie and place the bucket in the cave. Dad also taught Sky how to gather and transport water. Sky sometimes struggled to lift the heavy bucket and May would offer to help him. After the water was gathered, Mom would scale down and join the three by the sea to wash and splash in the shallow water pool between the large rocks.

Each day, Dad would give May and Sky a fishing pole to attempt to catch something for dinner. They used a lure as there was no live bait. Catching fish was not easy by the rocks with the waves breaking and crashing around. It was May who discovered the little crabs scurrying in the cracks in the rocks. They were much easier to catch and tasted great cooked on the fire. The hardest part was picking out the meat. Luckily, Mom had packed some forks and knives. Catching fish and crabs wasn't critical to survival as they still had the food supply in the cave, but it was important knowing how to find food if necessary. It also provided them with some exercise and an activity to pass the time. Mom and Dad reminded Sky and May every day to keep physically and mentally active.

During the time by the rocks, Sky and May learned to respect the ocean and keep an eye on the crashing waves. Falling off the rocks into the deep water could be fatal. The waves would tumble anything that fell in the water like clothes in a washing machine.

Unfortunately, May discovered this firsthand when a Breyer horse she was playing with on the rocks fell into the water. Instinctively, May reached down into the water to grab the horse before it sank in the ocean. As she leaned over, she slipped and fell headfirst off the rock into the water. Luckily, Dad was right there and grabbed her foot before her entire body went under. As he pulled her up to safety, May looked down to see the Breyer horse tumbling in the foam of the waves before crashing against the rock and sinking below the surface. May was devastated to lose her favorite horse, but her fear of what could have happened to her was stronger. While Sky wouldn't admit it out loud, he loved his sister more than anything and couldn't fathom losing her. He made her a drawing of the horse that night to put on the cave wall by her pillow. May looked at the drawing and smiled every night as she drifted to sleep.

After spending time by the rocks, the family climbed back up to the cave for lunch. This was usually something canned like tuna fish or spam, and fruit. In between lunch and dinner, they passed time down by the rocks, or in the cave reading, writing, drawing, or listening to music on Sky's headphones. Everyone tried to preserve the battery supply by limiting time on anything battery operated. Ensuring the walkie-talkies had batteries to operate was a top priority. Mom and Dad would try to communicate with anyone outside the cave on walkie-talkies each day to determine if it was safe to leave the cave, but all they heard was static.

Sky and May's favorite meal of the day was dinner. Mom would make something on the fire like pasta and sauce, mac and cheese, or ramen noodles. She would also make canned corn or carrots and canned pie filling or fruit for dessert. Before the cave, Sky and May were super picky eaters. In the cave, they learned to eat what Mom made. Mom would tease them that all it took was living in a cave with a limited food supply to get them to eat the meals she served without complaining. May and Sky would respond by listing the foods they were excited to eat as soon as they were back home. The list for both included milkshakes, chicken nuggets and cheeseburgers from McDonalds, pizza from anywhere, Starbucks pink drink, Doritos, chocolate chip cookies, banana bread, chocolate croissants, and pancakes.

In the evenings, the family sat around the fire reading, talking, writing, or drawing. They would even sometimes sing together. This would usually end with an argument over whether Mom or Dad had the worst voice. If May didn't like the songs or games played that night, she would let everyone know, she would shout with a frown, "These are the worst songs ever!" or "You cheated!" Mom and Dad were patient with May. Living in close quarters was not always easy without electronics or constant entertainment. Mom and Dad would remind Sky and May about the positives every day. "We are safe and healthy. We are together and have each other. We are not starving and have plenty. The view is amazing! We get to spend tons of time together and really connect." At first, Sky and May would roll their eyes and sigh when they heard these things. With just a glance at each other, Sky and May knew what the other was

thinking, "Are Mom and Dad crazy? Do they really think this is fun?" Oddly, as the days went by, Sky and May did start to enjoy some of the time in the cave together. They even found it relaxing at times without electronics to constantly check, places to go, and video game bosses to conquer. Sky sometimes would think it felt less stressful and more peaceful in the cave. However, they all knew, or hoped, the cave was temporary.

At night, Sky's mind often drifted to Minecraft Survival mode and thinking about creative ways to solve problems and build worlds. He also thought about the type of video games he wanted to create and the type of bosses he would fight in them. While Sky thought about gaming, May would think about riding her favorite pony Charlie, and wondered if he was safe and if "normal" horses and ponies were surviving. In her dreams, she wondered if she could somehow train the mashups to be friends with humans and peacefully co-exist. She loved all animals, even those Sky called Black Wolf. Sky would constantly remind May: "The Black Wolf is dangerous and is not a friendly pet! It will hurt you. Please promise me you will never get close to one!"

CHAPTER 5

WEEK 3
DAY 22
IN THE CAVE

Sky looked at the chalk marks on the cave wall where they kept track of days in the cave. He counted twenty-two marks and realized they had been in the cave over three weeks. On this twenty-second day in the cave, May, Sky and Dad started their morning descent down to the rocks. It was a typical sunny morning and May was busy looking for crabs in the rocks. Sky was washing his face and Dad was filling up the water bucket for Mom to pulley up to the cave. Suddenly, a loud roaring sound exploded over the ocean and the seagulls started to squawk and fly away. They all stopped what they were doing and looked up towards the sound. As they squinted into the bright sun, a huge, black military helicopter cut through the sky. Just as quickly as it appeared, it flew high above the cliff and disappeared. It was their first encounter with the outside world since being in the cave.

They climbed quickly back up to the cave and Mom grabbed the walkie-talkies, eager for some news. Questions swirled around Mom's head. Where did the helicopter come from? Where was it going? Was this a good sign? Were the mashups under control? Could they leave the cave and return to normal life? By the look on Mom's face, Sky could tell the walkie-talkies were not providing any answers. As usual, it was just static. As a lawyer, Mom was used to solving problems and finding answers. Sky could see her frustration. She turned to Dad, "We need to find out what's happening out there. Maybe the military has eliminated the mashups and we can return. At a minimum, maybe we should venture up the cliff and look around. The helicopter seems like a good sign something is happening. Even if we find out it's not safe, we can at least pick up more supplies from the house at night and bring them back to the cave."

Dad was silent for a minute, taking it in. "One step at a time. I will climb up the cliff tomorrow and see if I can see anything from there and if it looks safe. If it does, you and I could leave at night and stay close to the coast and try to find out what is happening. I'm not sure we can make it to the house unless it's completely safe."

Sky and May were puzzled. Sky stammered, "You can't leave May and I in this cave alone? Are you crazy? What if Black Wolf finds you? What if you don't come back?" May was crying, "Don't leave us here. I won't let you." Mom and Dad looked at both and Mom promised: "We will not leave unless we know it's safe. How will we ever get back home again if we don't leave this cave? We need to try." Sleep did not come easy to anyone that night. They were all worried but also anxious to see what Dad would find in the morning and whether that would mean Mom and Dad left at night.

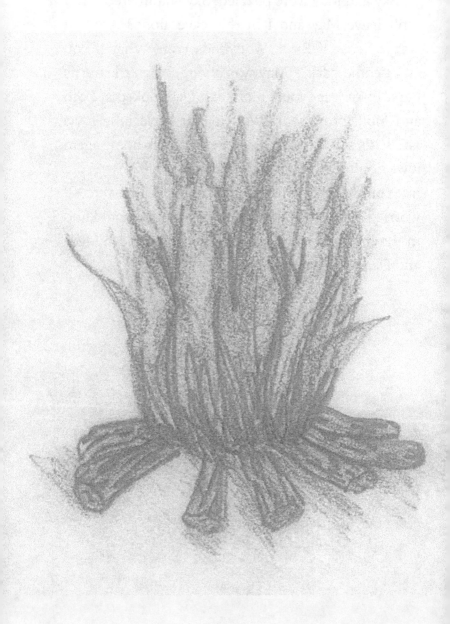

CHAPTER 6
WEEK 3
DAY 23
SEARCHING FOR
ANSWERS

They all woke up early as the sun was rising above the ocean and casting tiny sparkling white lights on the water. After breakfast, Dad was ready to climb up the cliff to take inventory of what was happening on the outside. While May and Sky were nervous for his climb, it was not because of the possibility of a climbing accident or encountering a mashup. Both of those scenarios were unlikely given Dad was a skilled climber and mashups appeared to avoid the rocky cliff and coastal terrain. Instead, May and Sky were nervous Dad would not encounter anything alarming and would deem it safe enough to travel with Mom at night.

As Mom, May and Sky stared into the sun at the top of the cliff, they could see the bottom of Dad's shoes as he swiftly climbed to the top of the cliff. At the top, he briefly stopped to look around and then hoisted himself on to the top ledge of the cliff and disappeared from sight. The cave remained silent as they waited for a sign from him or a sound. It seemed like time stood still. He was likely gone ten minutes, but to Sky and May, it felt like an hour. After what seemed like a long time, Mom, Sky and May saw small pebbles tumble past the cave entrance and heard Dad start his descent back down to the cave. As Dad entered the cave, Sky and May gave him a hug and Mom handed him a water.

Dad, breathing heavily from his climb, took a drink of water, and then described what he saw: "I did not see any mashups or people. I looked all around through the binoculars and could see only birds, a 'normal' red fox, and the empty coastline and marshes. I could hear some engines in the distance, but I couldn't tell how far they were or where they were. Nothing seemed out of place or different from other times I have been to this cave in the daylight. I did see a small boat washed up along the rocks further south, but I didn't see any people in or around it." His look turned serious. "Sky and May, I think it's safe for your Mom and I to leave tonight just to try and get a better sense of what is happening out there and gather some additional supplies from the house, if we can make it that far. It will likely take us three hours to walk to the house, two hours to gather supplies from the house, and then a three-hour walk back here. If we leave as soon as dark falls, we should make it back by morning."

While Mom did not want to leave the kids, she knew they would be safer in the cave. She looked at Sky and May and spoke as calm and steady as possible. "If for any reason we are not back tomorrow, do not leave this cave other than to climb down to the rocks for water and to wash. We will come back for you no matter what happens."

Sky and May did not want to hear this. Sky was scared and angry. "Why can't we go with you? Why would you leave us here? What if you don't come back?" May was upset and nodded her head at Sky, agreeing with him.

Dad calmly explained, "We can move more quickly without you and May," Dad explained calmly, "and there is no reason to risk either of you getting hurt. You will both be safe here. Mom and I will take knives, lighters, some food, and water, and will stick to the coastline. We will be careful." Mom always had to add something positive. "On the bright side," she said, "we can grab another Breyer horse from the house for May and some more batteries, books, and paper for Sky to draw and write. And maybe some Coke and candy, if we can find some at the house."

Mom hoped the house would be the same as they left it that night and not torn apart by mashups or people looking for food or shelter.

At dinner, Mom made everyone say something they loved about each other. Sky thought it was cheesy but didn't really have a choice in participating. Mom started the conversation, "Sky is gifted, May is brave, and Dad is strong." Dad was second. "Sky is kind, May is caring, and Mom is generous." May went next. "Mom and Dad are nice; Sky is funny and my hero." Sky was last and it took him a couple of minutes. He hated sharing feelings and did not enjoy this at all. It did make him feel good to hear what others had to say about him and was surprised May called him her hero. Being a hero also came with some additional responsibility with Mom and Dad leaving tonight. Sky said, "Mom is smart, Dad is good at stuff like climbing and making fires and May is ... my sister and ... pretty cool but loud." May's eyes lit up. If Sky thought she was pretty cool, then she must pretty cool. Sky wanted to move past all this lovey-dovey stuff, and he was glad when Dad changed the conversation.

Dad took Sky around the cave and reminded him where important things were like the first aid kit, supplies, lighters, batteries, etc. Sky knew all this, but Dad felt better reminding him. Dad also made

Sky walk him through how to start the fire, how to put it out, the safe way to climb to the rocks and back. He also told May to listen to Sky as he was in charge and made Sky and May promise not to fight or argue. Instead, they needed to work together and get along. Sky and May both rolled their eyes. Of course, they didn't plan to fight or argue; it sometimes just happened. They did agree to do their best.

As his responsibility sunk in, Sky felt far older than ten. He thought this must be what an adult feels like. He decided it wasn't fun and he was looking forward to being ten again when his parents returned. He hoped it would be very soon.

As darkness started to fall, the family hugged for a long time. Sky and May watched as Mom and Dad climbed out of the cave and up the cliff. They soon disappeared in the darkness.

CHAPTER 7

MOM
&
DAD

As Mom and Dad reached the top of the cliff, they were careful to quickly back away from the steep drop off overlooking the rocks. It was dark, but the moon was bright. They were both carrying a large backpack with supplies for a week, just in case things did not go as planned. They each had a flashlight, batteries, water, lighter, matches, blanket, tarp, knife, walkie-talkies (in case they could get them to work), food, a first aid kit, paper, and pens. They brought the paper and pens to record their journey and any mashups encountered or other critical information they could gather. Hopefully, the journal would describe that life was back to normal, no mashups anywhere, and the family could return home. Luckily, they had not set such high expectations.

While they desperately wanted to return to the

cave and Sky and May, they knew they had to start moving and getting answers. As they walked, they kept close to the coast but away from the rocky, slippery ledges. They did not speak to ensure they could hear everything around them and be completely aware of their surroundings. At this point, they did not see anything of concern. Their plan was to walk three hours to the house unless it became too dangerous. They couldn't risk anything happening to them with Sky and May back in the cave and depending on their safe return. Mom and Dad were both on edge and jittery but the constant moving, listening, and surveying the area kept their minds occupied.

About thirty minutes into their trip, Mom stumbled over something hard and fell forward onto the sandy gravel, scraping her knee and landing on her elbows in a sticky, wet puddle of liquid that smelled terrible. She let out a yelp as she slipped and landed. Before Dad could even kneel down to check on her, Mom scrambled back up and away from the foul-smelling puddle. Her hands and elbows were coated in the dark liquid and she whispered to Dad, "I'm ok but I cut my knee badly and need a bandage and there is something all over my hands and elbows from the fall. It smells horrible." Dad quickly took out his flashlight and aimed it at her knee. She was right, it was a bad cut and ideally, should have been stitched up. He did what he could with the first aid kit. He then aimed the light on her hands which appeared a blackish red color, and then on the ground. As soon as they saw the ground, they both jumped back.

The ground was covered with blood and a large animal carcass. Mom had tripped over the leg bone of the carcass. Dad quickly shined the flashlight around them to make sure there was no immediate threat near them. Obviously, something had killed this mashup based on the state of the mangled corpse. They just hoped it was not watching them right now. Seeing nothing, Dad looked closer at the carcass to try and determine what it was–it was the size of a large horse but much thinner and it had the head of some type of cat with two rows of long sharp teeth and paws instead of hooves. This was clearly some type of mashup. He would make sure and journal this later and let Sky select a name for this creature. While Dad was examining the mashup, Mom was busy trying to clean the gross blood from her hands and elbows. She used a wipe from her backpack and a little water. Her hands still smelled horrible but weren't as sticky. She just hoped the scent wouldn't attract any dangerous animals. Mom whispered to Dad, "The good news is that I can still walk, although my knee is throbbing, and I can't go fast.

The bad news is the mashups are not gone and they are close by unless a person killed this one and the government has the herds under control. Either way, this doesn't answer all our questions and I think we keep heading to the house for more answers. And the other bad news is that I smell like a dead mashup." Dad smiled and shook his head in agreement. "We will keep going but need to be careful. Walk behind me from now on and I will keep a light on our path."

While shaken up by the fall and the dead mashup, Mom and Dad started again on their journey. They did encounter two other similar carcasses about thirty minutes past the first one. Again, they did not see anything around the carcasses, so they kept moving. At this point, they were two hours into their walk and were optimistic they would reach the house in the next hour. They made occasional stops for a water break and snack, but otherwise kept in constant motion and focused on making it to the house. They weren't sure what they would find, but were hoping for the best and, at this point, becoming exhausted physically and mentally.

About three and a half hours after leaving the cave, Mom and Dad were approaching the house. When they were about thirty feet from the house, they ducked behind large grasses to take inventory of their surroundings and assess if it was safe to continue into the house. They carefully looked around with their flashlight and didn't see any mashups. The moonlight flickered on the canal across from the house on the right and they did not see movement on either side of the canal. They sighed with relief as their last sighting of mashup herds on the day they left was across the canal from their house. However, something was still not right and caused them both to pause before moving. Dad looked at Mom and nervously whispered, "Do you remember leaving a light on inside the house when we left?" Without hesitation, Mom answered "no". They looked at each other with fear and both had the same questions spinning in their head: "Is someone in the house? Did Sky or May accidentally turn on a light and we didn't know?" Dad finally whispered again, "Let's watch for a little while and see if there is any movement or sound from the house." Dad then looked around at the neighboring houses. He saw an occasional light in a window and did see cars in some driveways but did not see anyone or any movement. It was the middle of the night so either they were sleeping and things were fine or they had left their houses and forgot to turn out lights too.

After a half hour of crouching in the grasses, Mom and Dad began to hear rustling around them and some type of grunting and scratching. As the sounds seemed to be coming closer, they were suddenly surrounded by glowing yellow eyes in all directions. As the moon was bright, they could make out large dark shapes quickly approaching all around them. They were being surrounded and stalked by the mashups Sky called Black Wolf. Mom and Dad had no real weapons except knives, and even with weapons, they were no match for the number and size of the approaching mashups. They soon realized their only chance was to run for the house and hope the door was open. While they did have keys, it was unlikely there would be time to unlock the door. Without hesitation, Mom and Dad looked at each other and began to run to the front door. In an instant, the mashups were right behind them and they could hear growls and heavy breathing. As they raced to the front door, Mom tripped and Dad grabbed her hand to pull her towards the door. Suddenly, they were both slammed into the grass and the last thing they heard before losing consciousness was a crash and loud bang. Then, the world went black.

CHAPTER 8

THE HOUSE

Dad began to hear voices around him and started to make out blurry faces. He struggled to open his eyes and kept blinking to try and focus. Someone started to speak to him and was looking down on him and telling him to relax and that everything would be fine and to rest. He drifted in and out and finally opened his eyes and began to focus. The first person he could see was Mom lying next to him. She was breathing but not awake. He could see a bandage on her head and there was a scratch down her right cheek and her lip was swollen. His head started to spin, trying to figure out what happened and how they ended up here. He tried to sit up. Someone appeared next to him and told him to take it easy and rest. As he looked over, he was relieved to see Pop. Pop is Mom's dad and was nicknamed "Pop" by his grandkids, including Sky and May. Before he could start asking questions, Pep and Mom's sister, Ashe, appeared next to Pop. Pep is Mom's mom and also earned her nickname "Pep" from the grandkids.

Pop began explaining what happened. "Take it easy and don't move too quickly. You are lucky we were here and heard the mashups running across the lawn. We thought they were hunting animals until we looked out the window and saw you two running across the yard. As I opened the door, you were both knocked down by the mashups and were out cold from hitting the steps. The mashups gave you a few scratches and bites, but I fired a shot in the air and it startled them enough to back off and we dragged you in the house." He began tearing up. "Please tell me the kids are safe in the cave and weren't with you."

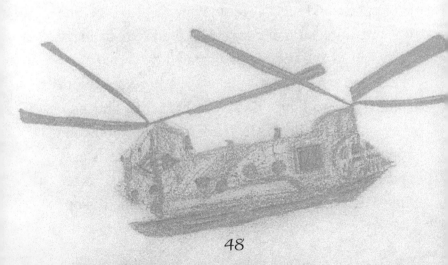

Dad nodded and all three let out a sigh of relief. Pop turned to Mom nervously. "We hope she wakes up soon. You have both been sleeping for eight hours." Dad tried to softly shake Mom and talk to her, but she didn't move.

Dad was worried about Mom but also still full of questions. He couldn't figure out why Pop, Pep, and Ashe were at the house. He knew the three of them and Ashe's kids had headed thirty miles outside of town to a military safe zone at the same time Mom, Dad, Sky, and May went to the cave. Nobody wanted to go to the safe zone as there weren't any guarantees there would be enough beds or how safe it would actually be there, however, there wasn't enough room in the cave for everyone and it would have been too hard for Pop and Pep to scale the cliff to go in and out of the cave. Besides, all of them thought the mashups would be under control and the area safe enough for them all to return to their homes quickly.

Pop could tell Dad was confused so he began to explain. "We were in the safe zone and didn't hear anything from you in three weeks. We didn't know if you were safe." Dad broke in. "Our walkie-talkies wouldn't work and we didn't have another way to reach out." Pop continued, "According to the news, they were flying military copters over this entire area and along the coast to determine the number of mashups, their location, and the best way to exterminate them. Apparently, they came up with a chemical harmful to solely the mashups based on their unique genetic mutations and safe for other animals. However, they are not sure of the impact on humans. The plan is to evacuate this entire area tomorrow, including the area near the cave, and start the chemical dusting in three days. They plan to do this everywhere by zone until the dangerous mashups are gone." Pop went on, "We left Ashe's kids in the safe zone and drove here today to find you and make sure you knew about the evacuation. We started with the house and when we realized you weren't back here, we were planning to go to the cave for you. Unfortunately, the mashups surrounded the house and have been stalking this area and we couldn't leave the house to get to the car safely."

Dad was suddenly very awake and trying to get up. "We need to head to the cave now for the kids and get out of here." Pop stopped him. "First, we need to get my daughter up and moving and come up with a plan to get the car without being overrun by mashups. Otherwise, none of us will survive. I have five shots left in this gun and not much else to handle these mashups."

"Do you have a cell phone?" Dad asked. "Won't the military or anyone help us out of here?" Pop broke in, "Everyone is on their own right now. There just aren't enough resources to handle these herds and get to everyone in time. Hopefully, after the chemical dusting, the herds will be gone or reduced enough for them to reach people. However, as the chemical dusting could hurt you and the kids, we can't wait until then." Dad was frustrated by the situation and anxious to get the kids to safety. He looked at Pop and said, "We need to come up with a game plan to get the kids and get to safety!"

CHAPTER 9

DAY & NIGHT 25 AT THE HOUSE

Mom did not wake up at all the first day at the house. She seemed to be in some pain and was mumbling in her sleep. In the middle of the night, Dad saw her eyes flicker open and then shut. He started talking to her and finally, after blinking several more times, she opened her eyes and seemed to focus. Dad brought her water and told her not to move right away. While Dad had suffered a bruise to the head when he was knocked down by the mashups, Mom had a large lump on her head, and cuts and bruising. She also had the cut on her leg from her fall. Mom grimaced as she sat up and drank the water. Dad had her take two Tylenol for the pain. As she gained her composure, she looked up to see Pop, Pep, and Ashe running into the room and smiling. They were so relieved she was awake, and she was excited and surprised to see all of them. Everyone started talking at once and catching up on what transpired and Pop repeated the information he had provided to Dad. Mom listened carefully and then began to panic when she realized she had been asleep for an entire day. She knew the kids were expecting them at the cave and they needed to get to them. Mom also knew she was in pain and walking back to the cave would be extremely difficult for her.

Dad started to fill Mom in on the game plan they had devised while she slept. "We plan to leave first thing in the morning as soon as there is enough light to see. We can take Pop's car to the cave, pick up the kids and head to the safe zone. To avoid being attacked by mashups as soon as we step outside, we plan to build and carry torches until we get to the car. We can also throw food out the windows on the back of the house furthest from the car to distract them and move them away from the front." Mom immediately thought of Sky playing Minecraft on his Xbox and using torches in the video game. This happy thought quickly evaporated as her mind switched over to the reality of their situation. She quickly began to poke holes in this plan. "How are we going to build torches? What if mashups surround the car? What if the roads are littered with carcasses and herds?" She could have kept going but Dad stopped her. "Pop only has a gun and not enough bullets and we have no other weapons of use against this many mashups. We know animals are fearful of fire and presumably, so are the mashups. We will break apart the chairs in the house and use the chair legs wrapped in cloth for our torch. We have oil lamps with oil to use on the cloth and plenty of lighters. We can each carry two torches and Pop can carry the gun. We can make a run for it." Mom frowned. "You didn't answer all the questions." Dad sighed. "I don't know if this will work or if the roads are safe and clear, but we need to try. What are the other options?" Mom thought for a few minutes. "There really aren't other great options. If we go with your plan, then we also need to bring some unlit torches along in the car and extra oil, just in case." Dad shook his head in agreement.

All five worked together to build the torches. With six dining room chairs, they were able to make twenty-four torches using the chair legs, dish rags, and oil. While they would only be carrying eight lit torches to leave the house, this would provide them with sixteen extra torches to take in the car, just in case they were needed. Dad packed the extra torches in a large travel bag. They also packed extra cans of food and water bottles, batteries, and clothes. Finally, Mom and Ashe grabbed cans of food they thought were smelly enough to attract the mashups and unlikely to be missed by the kids. These would be thrown out the window farthest from the car to distract the mashups. They hoped the food would keep the mashups preoccupied, even if only for a few minutes until they made it to the car. Mom and Ashe started emptying the cans into a large bowl so they could dump everything at once quickly. The smell of the mixture was terrible–sardines, olives, kidney beans, green beans, chili, diced tomatoes, and pickles. As Mom and Ashe began laughing at the odor rising from the bowl, Ashe pointed at Mom and said, "Speaking of bad smells, you need a shower!" Mom laughed in agreement as she remembered the terrible smell on her hands from falling over the carcass. It seemed like it happened ages ago, but it was just the prior night.

After showering, Mom joined everyone in the living room. She was stiff, bruised, and sore but at least clean. Ashe smiled at Mom. "You smell human again. The mashups won't confuse you with a dead animal." This made everyone laugh but didn't lighten the mood for long. With the dangerous morning mission looming a few hours away, nobody could sleep. Instead, everyone mentally prepared and waited for the first light of the day to appear.

CHAPTER 10

DAY & NIGHT 25 AT THE CAVE

With Mom and Dad gone, Sky and May had a restless sleep. When they woke on Day 25 in the cave and Mom and Dad weren't there, Sky tried to put on a brave face and keep May from worrying or asking more questions. Nervously smiling, he turned to May and said, "I bet Mom and Dad will return today! Let's eat breakfast and then go down by the rocks and get water and rinse off. We can even look for crabs to play with!" May wasn't hungry. While Sky had a can of fruit cocktail, May grew irritable. "This is the worst day ever," she said. "I miss Mom and Dad and I don't want to do anything and you can't make me! I hate this cave!" Sky tried to calm her down. "May, this does suck, but at least try doing something so you don't sit there grumpy all day." After some further coaxing, May agreed to climb down to the ocean rocks with him. Sky reminded her: "Do not go to close to the water and be careful." May rolled her eyes. "Stop being bossy," she replied.

Once down on the rocks, Sky and May noticed the seagulls circling overhead. The only other times Sky saw them do this was when the gulls spied a meal below. May looked up and asked, "What are they looking for?" Sky shrugged. He didn't see anything, so he walked further down to the rocks, closer to the water. Once he crossed over a group of sharp rocks, he peered over and saw a ball of white fur washed up on the rock closest to the water. He very slowly and carefully bent down to inspect the ball closer. May yelled at him, "Sky, you aren't supposed to be over there. If Mom and Dad find out you're that close to the water, you will be in so much trouble. Squealer!! Come back here!" Sky shouted back, "May, don't call me that! You are so annoying and loud! If you don't

58

stop yelling, I won't show you what I found over here." May, for once, stopped talking. Sky continued inspecting the fur ball. He thought it might be some type of very small animal but it was curled tight in a ball and he couldn't see a face. As he stared at the ball, he thought he saw some slight movement but he wasn't positive. While he didn't know what it was or whether it was alive, he did know that if left here, the sea gulls would swoop down and eat it or it would get swept back into the sea and drown. He also knew how much May loved animals of any kind and he thought this might cheer her up or at least keep her occupied. He weighed this against Mom and Dad warning them not to touch wild animals. Would Mom and Dad really be mad if the animal is the size of his palm and near death? After calculating the pros and cons, Sky decided to scoop the ball up in his bucket and see if he could move the ball around to get a better look.

He rolled the ball around carefully and he could see the fur was moving up and down slowly. He was fairly confident it was alive. With signs of life verified, he carried the bucket over to May who was by now growing impatient. She peered in and started excitedly peppering Sky, "What is it? Is it alive? Is it a baby? Is it a kitten, bunny, puppy, possum, squirrel, hamster, or rat? Whatever it is, can we keep it?" Sky cut her off. "May, relax. I don't know what it is, but I do think it's alive. Hand me your shovel so I can try to move it around and see what it is." May gladly handed him the shovel and stood wide-eyed as Sky gently used the end of the small shovel to pry open the small ball of fur. As soon as he touched it, a small squeaky noise came out of the creature. Sky and May were startled, but Sky continued to use the shovel to move it around, and slowly they were able to figure out what it looked like. Sky would later describe the creature in his journal:

The animal is covered in pure white fur. Once the fur dried, it was very fluffy and long. While it took some time, when it opened its eyes, one was brown and one was light blue. It has ears that are pointy and flop over at the top like puppy ears. It has a tail that reminds me of a kitten's tail (long and fluffy). The nose and mouth though are very odd. Both jut out and are boxy, almost like a pony with nostrils on the sides. The teeth are small and sharp like kitten teeth. It must be a mashup of different animals, maybe a cat, horse, and dog? It seems nice but it's too soon to tell for sure. Maybe it will stay small? I will call this type of mashup White Fox.

May instantly fell in love with the little creature. While she wasn't sure what it was, she was convinced it was part horse and she was ecstatic. "Sky, I can't believe it! It's the smallest, most amazing mini-horse ever! I think it's a girl so let's call it Prisma after my favorite Breyer horse. I am keeping her, she's mine!"

Sky was conflicted about the creature. He knew it was a mashup and knew they can be extremely dangerous. He had no idea where it came from, although he assumed it had somehow fallen in the water and been washed up on the rocks. He didn't know how big it would get or if it carried disease. What if it bit one of them? What would they feed it? Would Mom and Dad be mad? He then looked at the tiny creature that could fit in the palm of his hand and May's big blue eyes filled with joy and hope, and he knew he had to bring it up to the cave. When Mom and Dad came back, they could decide what to do.

After carefully scaling the sharp rocky wall, Sky and May settled back into the cave with Prisma still in the bucket. May started placing her hands towards the bucket to pick up Prisma, but Sky stopped her. "May, it could bite you or carry disease. Put socks on your hands to pick it up and don't put it near your face. And maybe put some water in front of it and fruit? I have no idea what else to feed it." May glared at Sky. "Seriously Sky, I know everything about horses. Waaayyy more than you. This is the coolest mini-horse, and horses like oats, so I'll feed her oatmeal." Sky sighed. "May, you don't even know what it is or if it's a horse, but go ahead and put some oats and water in front of it and see what it does."

May grabbed some socks and put them on her hands: she slowly and carefully picked up Prisma. As soon as she held the tiny creature in her hand, it looked at her but didn't move away or try to bite her. Instead, it looked up, made an odd sound, almost like a snort, and relaxed in her hands. It seemed to like the warmth she offered and was eager to dry off. She decided to let Prisma warm up and sleep before she tried feeding it. May wondered if Prisma had a family and missed them like May missed her Mom and Dad.

It wasn't until after lunch that Prisma woke. May immediately poured a little water into a bowl and laid some oats on the floor next to it. She set Prisma down in front of both. Prisma was very wobbly in standing on the four tiny legs and even fell down several times. After a few minutes, it was able to stabilize itself and start sniffing the feast May had set up. Sky and May stared at Prisma the whole time, hoping it would eat and drink something. They knew it needed to eat to get strength. To their relief, the little animal started to lap up the water. After drinking, it licked at the oats. As the oats stuck to Prisma's tongue, Prisma would then lick up more water to turn the oatmeal to mush before swallowing it. After expending so much energy on the feeding, Prisma slowly moved toward May and laid down against her leg and feel asleep again. May's eyes sparkled. "Sky, she thinks I'm her mom. She is so cute." Sky smiled and was relieved and happy May was preoccupied and happy. He then warned May: "Mom and Dad may not let you keep it when they come back so don't get too attached." He immediately regretting saying this as May started to tear up. "I want to keep Prisma. She needs a family. And when are Mom and Dad coming back? They are supposed to be here by now." Sky comforted her. "May, they will be back very soon and maybe they will like Prisma too." Sky kind of liked the creature too, but he was also a little scared of not knowing what it was or what it would become someday.

As the sun went down, Sky made dinner for May while she fed Prisma again. After dinner, Sky challenged May to a drawing challenge. "Let's see who can come up with the best drawing of what Prisma will look like grown up." May thought this was a great idea. After a half hour, May held up her drawing. It showed a fluffy white little horse the size of a cat on a leash held by May. Sky laughed and held up his drawing. May stared at it for a few minutes looking concerned. "Why is Prisma so big in your drawing with sharp teeth and a scary look?" Sky looked at her. "May, Prisma could end up big and scary. I know what other mashups look like and some are terrifying." May didn't like his answer. "Sky, you are so weird. Prisma is not like them. Look how little and cute!" Sky hoped she was right, but he was skeptical. Mom and Dad would know what to do. If only they would come back.

Sky and May went to sleep that night with Prisma sleeping on a towel in May's backpack, next to her. May left a little opening at the top for Prisma to get air and peek out. Sky had convinced May to put her in the backpack instead of right next to May in case Prisma wobbled to the cave opening and fell out

while they were sleeping. Even though they were worried about Mom and Dad, Prisma had offered enough distraction that both slept more soundly that night. However, it wasn't long before they were abruptly woken up, right after sunrise, by loud voices and people surrounding them in the cave.

CHAPTER 11

DAY 26
ESCAPE

As soon as the sun began to rise, Mom and Ashe went upstairs to the second-floor window furthest from their escape route with the stinky brew of food to distract the mashups. As they went up the stairs, Dad, Pop, and Pep began lighting the eight torches they would carry out to the car. The remaining torches were in the backpacks they would carry to the car. Ashe and Mom opened the window and threw the food as far out as they could. Immediately, they shut the window and ran down the stairs to join Dad, Pop, and Pep. Dad handed Mom and Ashe two torches each to carry. Pop carried the gun with the remaining shots, and Dad and Pep each carried two torches and backpacks.

On a three count, Dad clicked the car key button to unlock the car doors and opened the front door.

As soon the door swung open, they could all hear rustling sounds and noises from the other side of the house. Luckily, they didn't see any mashups at this point. As they moved towards the car, Ashe shouted, "Watch out! I see at least four mashups on the other side of the car and more in the bushes!" Pop fired a warning shot in the air and the group began to move quickly to the car. Ashe, Mom, Dad and Pep formed a close circle back-to-back and swung the torches around. They heard the mashups closest to the car began to snarl and could see glowing eyes and sharp teeth. As they got closer, they realized the enormous size of the mashups. Dad reached the car first just as a mashup lunged toward him over the car roof. Dad threw his flaming torches at the mashup and it growled and jumped back. Dad was able to swing the driver's side door open and crawl in. Behind him was Ashe and she quickly opened the back door, dropped her lit torches, and scurried across the seat and then over the center console into the front seat next to Dad. Next was Pep. She threw her torches towards mashups starting to surround them and threw herself into the back seat. As Mom went to climb in the back seat next, a mashup lashed at her and scratched her leg with sharp nails. Pop fired a shot at it and it scurried away. Mom tossed her torches towards the mashup and made it into the back seat. Pop was last to get in the car and used his final bullets to scare away the herd that was rapidly growing around the car. Dad had started the car as soon as he got in and was ready to hit the gas pedal as Pop closed the back door.

Dad reversed and accelerated quickly. He then put the car in forward and started speeding away from the mashups. Pop, Pep and Mom turned around in the back seat and could see the sheer volume of mashups left behind and were grateful to be in the car heading away. Some of the creatures were attempting to chase them, but the car was leaving them behind, churning up dust and gravel as Dad sped down the road. Mom could feel blood running down her leg and quickly pulled a large bandage out of a backpack to stop the bleeding. At the same time, Pop and Pep grabbed four of the extra torches from the backpacks and passed them around to Mom and Ashe just in case they needed to quickly light and use them.

As Dad continued racing down the road, they noticed military helicopters flying in the distance. They knew these would be used for spraying the chemicals in the following days. While they didn't see other cars on the winding road along the coast, they did see several mashup corpses. They also saw several mashup herds. At one point, Dad was forced to slow down to zigzag around a tree and several mashups in the road. He honked to scare them and they backed away from his path. After a stressful drive, they began to approach the closest parking area to the cave.

As soon as they arrived, Dad stopped the car and they looked out the windows to make sure they didn't see any mashups close by. The coast seemed clear, so Pop, Pep, and Ashe each grabbed a torch and lit them outside the car. Mom and Dad ran to the top of the cliff to begin their descent to the cave entrance while Pop, Pep, and Ashe stood in a circle with the torches to ward off any approaching mashups. Mom and Dad were slow in scaling the cliff to the cave due to their injuries. Fortunately, they made it to the cave and as they went through the entrance, they were so relieved to see May and Sky sleeping and safe. However, they didn't have time to enjoy the reunion; they had to quickly wake them and get them to the car. Mom and Dad called to the kids and nudged them awake.

The kids abruptly woke up and were scared at first at the commotion. As soon as they realized it was Mom and Dad, they started smiling and Mom and Dad gave the kids hugs. Mom sounded anxious and said, "We can't explain anything now, but we need you both to quickly grab your backpacks and you have two minutes to pack what you need. We need to leave the cave now!" May and Sky could sense the urgency and they both ran around quickly grabbing what they could. Sky grabbed his journals and pens, and May grabbed her backpack with Prisma inside and carefully placed two Breyer horses in the backpack. She wanted to tell Mom and Dad about Prisma, but everything happened so fast and she was afraid they wouldn't let her bring the little horse along. Sky was also in a hurry and focused on packing what he needed. After the two minutes, Dad was first up the cliff, followed by Sky, May, and then Mom. Both kids climbed much more easily than Mom and Dad. As they got to the top of the cliff, the kids saw torches and three people standing ahead. Mom and Dad told the kids to run quickly towards the group. As soon as the kids got close enough, they were excited to see Pep, Pop, and Ashe. The kids got in the car first and Dad drove again, with Ashe in the passenger seat and Mom, Pop, and Pep in the back with the two kids. They were crowded in, but nobody cared. They were just relieved everyone was safe and on their way to safety.

Immediately, both kids started peppering everyone in the car with questions, and May told Mom and Dad she was angry with them for not coming back earlier. Mom calmly cut them off and began to fill them in on the last days events. The kids listened with wide eyes and terror, and then it turned to excitement as they were told they were heading to the safety zone and would see their cousins, Noelle and Cam. The past month was the longest the four cousins had ever gone without seeing each other. They normally played almost every day and shared everything. They were not just family but also best friends. Sky couldn't wait to let them know about the cave, and May was excited to play horses with Noelle and share her new secret hidden in her backpack.

Mom and Dad asked the kids about their time alone in the cave. Sky began by boasting about what an amazing job he did watching over May while they were gone and then he started to talk about finding Prisma. Mom, Dad, Pop, Pep, and Ashe were eager to hear about Prisma and Sky showed them his journal picture of the little creature. Sky thought May had left Prisma in the cave and didn't realize May had her tucked in her backpack. May really wanted to reveal Prisma but feared the reaction from Mom and Dad. Before May could say or do anything, Dad said. "Sky, you are lucky Prisma didn't bite either of you. It could have been dangerous. I'm glad you are both safe and you left it behind in the cave. I'm sure they wouldn't let us in the safety zone with a mashup. They are planning to get rid of the mashups with the chemicals." As soon as May heard this, she knew she couldn't tell them about Prisma in her bag. They would make her let Prisma go and Prisma was so small, May was sure she would get hurt out here alone. Plus, May couldn't wait to show Prisma to Noelle. She knew Noelle would fall in love with her. May sat in the car in silence and hoped Prisma would sleep the whole ride and not make a sound.

The car ride felt like an eternity for everyone. They were completely exhausted by the time they arrived at the safety zone checkpoint. Luckily, Ashe, Pop, and Pep had proper documentation for the safety zone, and all Mom and Dad had to do was show identification for themselves and for May and Sky and sign papers showing they were all related. This would ensure they could enter the safety zone and be placed with Pop, Pep, Ashe, Noelle, and Cam. Living quarters would be tight, but they were happy they would be together and safe. Prior to entering the safety zone, the officer in charge confiscated all the remaining torches and Pop's gun for safety purposes. They also asked about the contents of each backpack but didn't search May or Sky's backpacks. May was relieved and continued to keep Prisma a secret.

CHAPTER 12

THE AFTERMATH

U pon entry into the safety zone, Mom, Dad, Sky, and May followed Ashe, Pop, and Pep to their temporary living quarters. As soon as Cam and Noelle spotted everyone, they started to jump up and down and ran over to the group to give hugs. The kids all started talking at once and telling each other about the crazy events leading up to their reunion. Noelle noticed May was a little quiet and took May by the hand and showed her the bunk bed where she would sleep. May whispered to Noelle that she had something to show her but needed a place where they could be alone. Noelle yelled to Ashe and Mom that she was going to show May the little playground through the exit door. Noelle had a hiding spot behind a large tree where she liked to read and get a break from the cramped living quarters.

As soon as the girls were outside behind the tree, May told Noelle, "Whatever you do, don't yell or draw attention. You have to promise to keep this a secret." Noelle held up her pinky and made a pinky promise to May. May slowly opened her backpack and Prisma peeked out. May could tell she was hungry and knew they had to feed her and let her move around. Noelle's eyes were huge and she started to smile. She whispered, "It is sooo cute, but what is it and where did it come from? It kind of looks like a horse but is really small. Is it a mashup?" May explained how they found Prisma and then told Noelle how she snuck Prisma from the cave. May told Noelle, "I really don't know what it is or how big it will grow. I think it's a tiny horse, but Sky warned me it could become a dangerous mashup. I don't believe him though. If we tell anyone about Prisma, they will take her away and hurt her." Noelle shared a love of animals with May, and she agreed to keep the secret. The two girls knew this was their biggest secret to date and keeping this secret was risky. However, they agreed this secret was worth keeping.

May then asked Noelle if there was water or food they could sneak to Prisma. Noelle told her to wait and she ran inside to grab a banana left over from lunch. She also filled up a bottle with water. She brought them outside and handed them to May.

Prisma was so hungry she ate the entire banana out of May's hand by taking little bites. May then poured some water in Prisma's mouth and Prisma drank half the bottle. Noelle looked concerned. "May, where are we going to keep Prisma and where will she sleep? We can't risk anyone hearing or seeing her." May had not thought that far ahead and she didn't have an answer. Noelle asked to hold Prisma while they came up with a plan. As soon as Noelle picked her up, Prisma curled in a ball to sleep. Noelle looked at May. "Maybe we can use a cardboard box as a home for Prisma and hide her behind this tree. We can hang out here as much as possible and hide Prisma in our backpacks whenever we can. They have a ton of cardboard boxes out back by the dumpsters. If anyone asks, we can tell them we are building a small barn for our Breyer horses." May thought this was a great idea and the girls went in search of a box.

While the girls hatched their plan to hide Prisma, Mom and Dad went to the medical facility at the shelter for treatment for their injuries. They were both treated with antibiotics and received testing to ensure the bites and wounds from the mashups did not transmit any diseases. They were bandaged and told to rest. While they rested, Ashe, Pop, and Pep gave Sky and Cam a snack and some water. May and Noelle told everyone they were busy "building a Breyer barn" out of a cardboard box.

After a few days of bunking together with limited space, everyone - except May and Noelle - was becoming very anxious for news of the mashups and eager to return home to normalcy. May and Noelle seemed to be enjoying their time playing outside behind the tree. Everyone thought they were just having fun with their Breyer horses. On the fourth day of their arrival at the safe zone, Mom and Dad finally received some news during a follow-up appointment at the medical facility. According to the doctor, they had just received word that the chemicals had destroyed sufficient numbers of dangerous mashups and crews had worked night and day to remove remnants of the mashups. As the chemicals sprayed had already been tested for human safety, there were no concerns with people returning to those areas. They estimated people would be allowed to return to their homes, or what was left of them, in the next two days. This news was a huge relief and the remaining days in the safety zone flew by.

As Mom, Dad, Sky, May (with Prisma safely hidden in her backpack), Pep, Pop, Cam, Noelle, and Ashe began their journey home, emotions were mixed. There was happiness, excitement, and optimism for the future. Everyone was grateful to be alive and together. However, questions and concerns weighed heavily on everyone.

Were their homes damaged or destroyed by the mashups? Would everything go back to how it was before they left? Were the mashups gone? Had some escaped the chemicals? Were humans safe?

May and Noelle had additional concerns. Where would they hide Prisma at home? What would happen if anyone found Prisma? What if Prisma grew big and dangerous?

Some of these questions they would soon have answers to. The remainder of the answers would take time and patience to determine.

As they passed by the road leading to the coast and the cave, Sky looked out the window and smiled. He knew there were questions and challenges ahead, but he had learned so much from his experience in the cave. Sky appreciated the unbreakable bond of his family and realized strength, love, courage, hope, and happiness are possible even during the darkest times.

ABOUT THE AUTHOR

Kimberly Andrascik is an attorney, author and owner of a home renovation company. She currently lives with her husband and children in Berlin, MD. She began writing in order to inspire her children to take their ideas and imagination and create stories. Her motto is: ***Dream It, Be It, Start It, Finish It!***

CPSIA information can be obtained
at www.ICGtesting.com
Printed in the USA
BVHW072024190122
626641BV00002B/23